Starfall

Diana Kolpak
Photographs by Kathleen Finlay

Red Deer PRESS

Meera imagined blue skies,
warm sunshine,
laughter . . .

A snowflake landed on her nose.

She sighed.

"There are no stars to hold up my dreams.
The stars fell, then the snow began to fall
and now there's just me."

Her shoulders sagged.

"I have to wake up the stars. But how?"

Meera began to walk.

A thousand heartbeats . . .
A thousand breaths . . .
A thousand steps . . .
Her feet grew heavy.

"Endless snow.
Endless, endless cold."

She stopped.
The wind whispered:
"Stay where you are. Forget the stars."

"No." Meera forced her cold feet forward.
"I must go on."

Crunch, crunch, crunch.
She walked and walked until
she reached the top of a high, high hill.

"What's that?"
Meera ran.

She slipped and tumbled and slid
and stopped, breathless,
in front of a Fortune Teller's booth.
Inside was a woman carved from wood.

"Hello," Meera said.
"Please tell me how to wake the stars."

Click . . . creak . . . whirr . . .
The figure began to speak:
"The Dream Tree holds the key
to what you seek.
Follow your heart to find the way."
Whirr . . . clack . . . clunk.

"Wait! Where is this tree?"

The figure was silent.

"Follow my heart."

Meera turned to her left.
"This way."

She walked for a thousand heartbeats,
a thousand breaths,
a thousand steps.

The Dream Tree!

"Where are the stars?"
Meera asked.

She waited.
She yawned.
Her eyes drooped shut.

A voice rustled like fallen leaves:
"The stars are waiting for you.
Three things will help you find them:

"Believe."

"Be brave."

"Shine."

Meera's eyes popped open.

"I need to find the door."

She shook the snow from her shoulders
and started to walk.

She climbed every hill.
She searched all the shadows.
She peered into the wind.

Her feet grew numb.
Her fingers ached with cold.
"There's nowhere left to look."
Tears froze to her cheeks.

The waves murmured:
"You'll never find what you're looking for."

"Believe."

Meera took a deep, deep breath.
"I believe I can find the door."

She turned around.

And there it was.

Meera laughed.

She knocked on the door.
Nothing happened.

She grasped the handle
and pulled . . .

. . . and disappeared.

"Hello."

Meera opened her eyes.
A boy was looking down at her.
"I'm Teeg," he said.

"I'm Meera."

In the sky she saw a twinkling light.
"A star!"

But the star flickered and fell into the water,
then it was gone.

Meera's heart sank.

"They've all fallen now," Teeg sighed.
"I was trying to fish the stars from the water
but pulled out you instead."

"I'm trying to find the stars, too."

A cold wind rippled across the waves.

Shoosh, shoosh, shoosh.

"Von," Teeg called out,
"I caught a star-seeker. Her name is Meera."

"Hello," said Meera.
"I need to find the man who juggles fire."

"Hop in," Von said, "I'll take you to Olly,
he'll show you the way."

"You'll find them, Meera, I know it."

"Thank you Teeg. Goodbye."

Teeg kissed Meera's cheek.

A thousand heartbeats…
A thousand strokes…
Night gave way to misty dawn.
"Ahoy there," a voice called from the shore.

"Olly, this is Meera.
She needs to get to the Fire Juggler."

Olly shrugged. "All paths lead to the Juggler.
Some are more dangerous than others."

"Well," asked Meera, "how can I tell
which are safe and which are dangerous?"

"I didn't say any were safe."

Meera looked at the sky.
Thick grey clouds twisted and swirled, blocking out the sun.

"The stars have fallen, the snow will follow.
I must choose a path."

Von pulled Olly out of the tree.
"If Meera is willing to try, we should be willing to help."

So Meera, Olly and Von set out together.

The path grew darker,
the wind blew colder
and their hearts grew heavier.

A whisper snaked through the forest:
"Round and round and round we go…"

Von and Olly stopped.

"Come on," Meera said.

"We can't." Olly shuddered.
"No one gets past the Spinner."

The whisper grew louder:
"Twist and twirl, grasp and snatch.
Step forward and you're mine."

Nobody moved.

"Please let me pass."
Meera's voice sounded very small.
"I have to wake the stars."

The Spinner hissed,
"Foolish girl with a foolish dream.
You'll never find the stars."

"Be brave."

Heart pounding, Meera stepped forward.
"Foolish? For loving the stars?
Foolish for daring to dream?
You are foolish to think you can stop me."
She walked straight toward the Spinner.

Poof.

The Spinner vanished.

A snowflake fell,
then another . . . and another.

"Von, Olly, we've got to hurry."

"Look." Olly pointed up the path.
Firelight flickered through the trees.

They ran toward the spinning lights.

"Is this the way to the stars?"
Meera asked.

The Juggler bowed his head.
"Only one may enter."

Meera hugged Von, then Olly.
"Thank you. Goodbye."

Meera stepped into the dark,
down and down and down
a thousand steps,
and then a thousand more.

"Hello? Is anybody there?"

"Welcome."
A tall, tall man stepped into the lamplight.
He opened a very, very short door.
"After you."

Meera ducked through.
Her eyes lit up in wonder.

"Who are they?" Meera asked.

"Dreamers,"
the tall, tall man replied.
"One of them is waiting for you."

"The one I'm looking for?"

"I knew you'd find the stars,"
the Fortune Teller said.

Meera knelt beside her.
"But I haven't . . ."

"You've gathered them along the way:
the kiss on your cheek,
the strength in your steps,
the hope in your heart."

"The stars . . . they are in me?"

The Fortune Teller smiled.
"Let's get you where you need to be."

Meera laughed and laughed,
flying higher and higher
and higher

until . . .

She was

Light.
Water.
Sky.

"Shine."

Snow swirled at Meera's feet.

In her hands a tiny star
shone bright and warm.

Meera lifted the star above her.
She stood on tiptoe,
reaching as high as she could
and let it go.

The star floated up . . . up . . . up . . .

On every side of Meera
the snow began to glow.

Thousands of stars broke free of the ice
glimmering, twirling, dancing...
filling the night sky with light,
and melting the winter away.

For Matias, Loïc and David — KF

For my parents, who let me be a dreamer,
and for Michael, who holds up my dreams. — DK

Performers: Paul Babiak, R.J.L.R. Baird, Erin Bouvy, Ben
Burland, Eli Chornenki, Kaylen Davidson, Jennifer
Georgopoulos, Diana Kolpak, Jeff Krahn, Peter Loung, Dave
McKay, Kate Mior, Claire Ness, Giovanni Salvia, Lindsay
Stephens and David Tomlinson.

Special thanks to Peter Loung, Clair Ness, David Tomlinson
and Zero Gravity Circus.

Fortune Teller booth created by R.J.L.R. Baird

A portion of the creators' proceeds from Starfall will be donated
to support local therapeutic clown programs.

Published by Red Deer Press, A Fitzhenry & Whiteside Company
195 Allstate Parkway, Markham, ON L3R 4T8
www.reddeerpress.com

Published in the United States by Red Deer Press, A Fitzhenry & Whiteside Company
311 Washington Street, Brighton, Massachusetts, 02135

Edited for the press by Kathy Stinson
Cover and text design by Blair Kerrigan/Glyphics
Cover images by Kathleen Finlay
Printed and bound in Hong Kong, China by Sheck Wah Tong in September 2011, job #56604

5 4 3 2 1

We acknowledge with thanks the Canada Council for the Arts, and the Ontario Arts Council for their support of our
publishing program. We acknowledge the financial support of the Government of Canada through the Canada Book Fund
(CBF) for our publishing activities.

 Canada Council   Conseil des Arts
for the Arts   du Canada

 ONTARIO ARTS COUNCIL
CONSEIL DES ARTS DE L'ONTARIO

Library and Archives Canada Cataloguing in Publication
Data is available on file, ISBN 978-0-88995-469-4.

Publisher Cataloging-in-Publication Data (U.S.)
Kolpak, Diana.
    Diana Kolpak ; photography by Kathleen Finlay.
[48] p. : col. photos. ; cm.
Summary: The stars have fallen, bringing endless winter. Guided by a dream tree,
a clown sets off on a journey through a magical landscape to find them.
ISBN: 978-0-88995-469-4
1. Fantasy fiction – Juvenile literature. I. Finlay, Kathleen. II. Title.
[E] dc22   PZ7.K6573St   2011